Quentin Blake
& André Bouchard

DADDY LOST HIS HEAD

Red Fox

For Olivia

A.B.

DADDY LOST HIS HEAD
A RED FOX BOOK 978 1 862 30996 8

First published in France in 2008 as *La tête ailleurs* by Circonflexe
First published in Great Britain by Jonathan Cape,
an imprint of Random House Children's Books
A Random House Group Company

Jonathan Cape edition published 2009
Red Fox edition published 2011

1 3 5 7 9 10 8 6 4 2

Illustrations copyright © Quentin Blake, 2008
Text copyright © André Bouchard, 2008
Translation copyright © Quentin Blake, 2009
Copyright © 2008 by Circonflexe, *La tête ailleurs*

Red Fox Books are published by Random House Children's Books
61–63 Uxbridge Road, London W5 5SA

www.**kids**at**randomhouse**.co.uk
www.**rbooks**.co.uk

Addresses for companies within The Random House Group Limited can be found at: www.randomhouse.co.uk/offices.htm

THE RANDOM HOUSE GROUP Limited Reg. No. 954009

A CIP catalogue record for this book is available from the British Library.

Printed in China

Daddy had lost his head.

It was plain to see that there was nothing on his shoulders.

He kept bumping into things all over the house. When he broke a very old, ugly, expensive china ornament that Mum loved, we had to ask him to stay sitting down. Even without ears he could still hear her.

Once he was finally settled in his chair, he stayed there.
It was as if he had been unplugged. We took the opportunity
to go and look for his head.

First of all, Mum glanced quickly into every room in the house.
Then she looked again, this time more carefully. Finally, she even
searched in places she knew Dad's head could not have been.
In the end, she had to admit that we couldn't find it.

It was embarrassing not knowing where to look when we were talking to Dad. How were we going to explain to people that he had lost his head and we couldn't find it? Mum started to cry. She could imagine people saying, "Look at this careless woman who can't even find her own husband's head. What can she be like with her children's socks!" So my brother and I decided to make a head for Dad, so that people wouldn't say things like that, and make Mum cry.

Making a head for your dad is easy, especially if he doesn't look like a film star. First, you get lots of his old newspapers and roll them into a ball the size of his head. Next, you paint it the colour of his skin. When that's dry, you draw on his eyes, eyelashes and mouth.

Make the nose out of a potato. (If your dad's nose is bigger than that, you could always use part of a cauliflower.)

Paint the nose the same colour as the skin, but add a bit more red. Finally, if you have a dad who still has hair, all you need is some wool and some glue, and then that's it: you've done it!

Dad's head was finally ready. It was even better than the original.
It looked completely real – so much so that Mum said, "Brilliant!
You've found it!"

When we gave it a tap with a hammer to show her it was only paper, she fainted.

On Monday morning, Dad had to go to work. He jumped into the driving seat of the car, and Mum only just had time to get in beside him to help him steer. She left him at the entrance of his office, and he went in on his own, probably through force of habit.

You have to admit there were several advantages to Dad having lost his head. For instance, he didn't make an awful fuss if you did something really stupid.

He always agreed with Mum, and did all kinds of things for her. As he didn't have a brain to think for himself, she gave the orders and he obeyed.

It was really very useful for Mum. Dad was delighted to do the cooking, loved laying the table, adored doing the washing-up, and made a great job of the hoovering.

When he got tired, Mum filled him up
with mince and mashed potatoes.

We didn't look forward to bedtime though, because after Mum, it was Dad's turn to give us a kiss. It was horrible, because the paper scratched, and if you were stupid enough to kiss him back, the paint came off on your mouth.

But what was really brilliant for Mum was having a husband who didn't snore in bed any more.

Dad kept lots of his old habits though – things that grown-ups just do automatically. For instance, one morning we had to repaint his face just as he was setting off to the office, because he'd tried to shave it.

Another time he went out jogging and forgot his head...

Quick as a flash, Mum was on her bike. Freddy sprinted behind like a greyhound, while I stood on the back. It was my job to stick his head back on when we caught up with him. It was lucky we didn't meet anybody in the park that morning because we were a strange sight, all three of us in pyjamas chasing a man without a head…

We'd nearly reached the other side of the park when we finally stopped Dad. He tripped over a tree root and we fell on top of him.

We soon got everything back in order, except that Dad had a rather funny expression, because when I fell over I squashed his head a bit.

The fact that Dad did whatever he was told gave me and my brother an idea: if we took him to a big department store then he'd buy us anything we asked for. In no time we came up with a great way of doing this. Freddy hid under Dad's jacket, fastened in by a belt and braces, and imitated Dad's voice, speaking through an empty yoghurt pot.

We had it all worked out – I led Dad around by the hand, and Freddy talked to the sales people. We got Dad to buy us amazing things: a remote-control aeroplane, dolls, computer games, pedal-cars, two Zorro dressing-up sets, an electric train, a castle, a convertible to take my dolls out in, and terrific space-warriors with weapons everywhere – even in their pants.

While I was choosing a pink private jet so that my dolls could go on holiday, Freddy had fallen for a blue furry mammoth which was nearly life-size. He was so excited that he forgot to imitate Dad's voice and shouted, "That's for me!"

Once we got to the till, Dad's hand took his wallet out of his jacket pocket, and his credit card out of his wallet, and then – thanks to the Super Brilliant Force of Habit – he tapped his PIN into the machine. Apart from a bit of trouble getting the mammoth into our car, it was a complete success!

Another time, Mum arrived in the lounge in an evening dress, and with so much make-up on that she looked as if she was painted like Dad.

She wanted Dad to waltz with her, so he got up and took her in his arms, and they started to dance.

To begin with, she was very happy to be dancing with Dad. But
after a minute or two she started complaining that he was going
too fast; soon she was yelling for him to stop.

So he did. Mum staggered about in all directions before she sat down,
complaining that she had an awful headache. Dad was perfectly happy
– he didn't have a headache. Well, he wouldn't, would he?

And then, one day, Daddy came back with his REAL head! It turned out that he had left it at the office because he needed all of his brain to work on a project that was Ultrasupertopimportant.

Dad seemed to have no memory of the time he had spent without his head. And we didn't tell him about it. We were happy, because we had been missing Dad's real head. Especially since it contained his special recipe for chocolate cake and all the stories that he told in a deep voice at bedtime. When night fell, it was lovely for us to hear Dad's super snoring, capable of penetrating the thickest walls.

Mum must have missed it a lot.

As for the paper head, who knows where it is now.